For my grand-maman

First American Edition 1997 by Kane/Miller Book Publishers
Brooklyn, New York & La Jolla, California

Originally published in Canada in 1989 by
Stoddart Publishing Co. Limited, Toronto

For information contact:
Kane/Miller Book Publishers
P.O. Box 310529, Brooklyn, N.Y. 11231-0529

Library of Congress Cataloging-in-Publication Data

Gay, Marie-Louise.
Fat Charlie's circus / Marie-Louise Gay. — 1st American ed.
p. cm.
Summary: Fat Charlie's boasting gets him into a predicament in a tall tree,
but his grandmother saves him in a way that leaves his pride intact.
ISBN 0-916291-73-1
[1. Grandmothers—Fiction. 2. Pride and vanity—Fiction.] I. Title.
PZ7.G2375Fat 1997   [E]—dc20   96-38450

Printed and bound in Singapore by Tien Wah Press Ltd.
1 2 3 4 5 6 7 8 9 10

FAT CHARLIE'S CIRCUS

Marie-Louise Gay

A CRANKY NELL BOOK

Kane/Miller Book Publishers

Brooklyn, New York & La Jolla, California

Fat Charlie
loved the circus
more than
anything else
in the world.
He knew that
when he grew up
he would perform
in a circus.

Whenever his father said,
"Charles, clean up your room,"
Fat Charlie closed his bedroom door
and practiced his Lion-Taming Act.
His room got very messy.

If it was his turn to feed the goldfish,
Fat Charlie would train them
to jump through a hoop.
His cat thought it was a great act.
His mother made him mop the floor.

When he was told to hang up the wash,
Fat Charlie worked on his
Terrific Tightrope Act.
Until…

… Dorothy, his sister, decided to help.
Fat Charlie's mother had to wash
all the clothes again.

One day he juggled a set of plates
and smashed them to smithereens.
His parents got really fed up.
"That's enough! No more crazy
circus acts!"
Fat Charlie said nothing.
Fat Charlie knew what he would do.

He would perform the
greatest circus act ever.
He would show them!
He would climb to the top of the tallest tree
in the yard and dive into a small,
very small glass of water.
Fat Charlie's Daring Diving Act!
He would be famous!

"Silly!" said Dorothy.
"You'll break your leg!"
"No, I won't," said Fat Charlie
as he started climbing.
"You're nuts!" cried Dorothy.
"You'll smash your head!"
"No, I won't," said Fat Charlie
as he reached the first branches.
"You're crazy, Fat Charlie!
You'll probably drown!" yelled Dorothy.
"I'm going to tell mama!"
And she did.

The next morning, Fat Charlie
and his grandmother
practiced their Bicycle Balancing Act
all the way to the grocery store.
They were going to buy eggs.

"WAIT!" yelled Fat Charlie.
"Climb down with me. I'll help you."
His grandmother thought it over.
"O-o-oh, all right."
So Fat Charlie helped his grandmother
slide all the way down the tree.
"Thank you, Charlie,"
said his grandmother.
"I was a bit scared up there."
"Me too," said Fat Charlie.
And they both went into the house.

"GRANDMA!" said Fat Charlie.
"What are you doing up here?"
"I wanted to see the view," said his grandmother.
"So, Charlie, are you going to dive into the glass?"
"Not right now," mumbled Fat Charlie.
"Why don't we jump together?"
said his grandmother.
"You can't jump," said Fat Charlie.
"You'll break your leg!"
"No, I won't, said his grandmother
as she stood up on the branch.
"Don't jump, Grandma," cried Fat Charlie.
"You'll smash your head!"
"No, I won't," said his grandmother.
"I want to be famous too!"
And she leaned over.

Fat Charlie was all alone.
"What should I do?"
thought Fat Charlie.
"I'm too scared to dive.
I'm too scared to move.
Everyone will laugh at me."
Then he heard
a tiny whisper:
"Charlie..."

"Come down," said his mother. "It's time for supper."
"Yeah," said Dorothy, "spinach and carrots, dee-licious!"
"Come down this minute!" yelled his father,
"or you'll go to your room!"
"Yeah," said Dorothy, "forever."
"Come down, Charlie," said his grandmother. "Please."
Fat Charlie didn't answer. Fat Charlie didn't look down.
Fat Charlie was scared.
Soon there was a big crowd at the foot of the tree.
Everybody yelled, "Charlie, come down!
Come down, Fat Charlie!"
But Fat Charlie didn't come down.
Fat Charlie didn't budge an inch.
"I'm going to be famous," he said.
Finally everybody got tired of waiting
and they all went home
for supper.

Fat Charlie finally reached the top of the tree.
He looked down.
The glass was just a tiny speck.
"Uh-oh," whispered Fat Charlie.
Then his father, his mother, his grandmother
and his sister rushed out of the house.